Jasper and the
MAGPIE

Jasper and the
MAGPIE

Enjoying special interests together

Dan Mayfield

Illustrated by Alex Merry

Jessica Kingsley *Publishers*
London and Philadelphia

First published in 2015
by Jessica Kingsley Publishers
73 Collier Street
London N1 9BE, UK
and
400 Market Street, Suite 400
Philadelphia, PA 19106, USA

www.jkp.com

Library of Congress Cataloging in Publication Data
A CIP catalog record for this book is available from the Library of Congress

British Library Cataloguing in Publication Data
A CIP catalogue record for this book is available from the British Library

ISBN 978 1 84905 579 6
eISBN 978 1 78450 035 1

Printed and bound in China

Jasper really liked
shiny metals.

He loved that when the sun shone
Electrons danced reflecting light.

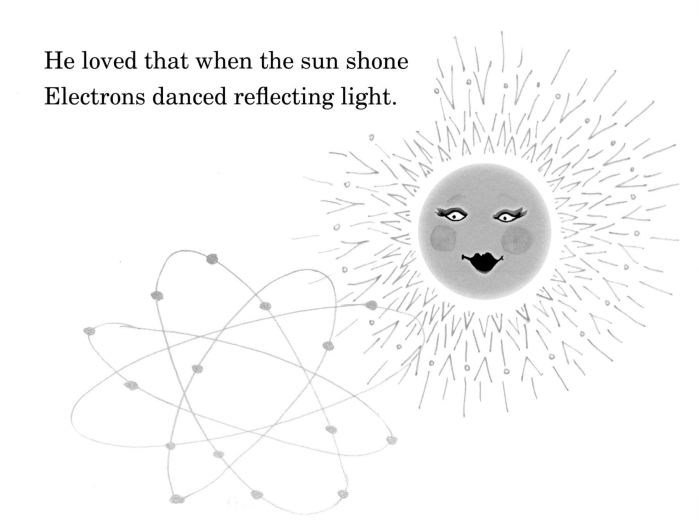

This made him feel safe and calm,
And helped him sleep at night.

In his science books
Jasper read about them all,
Like zinc, gold, bronze and silver;
He knew lots about tin foil.

But he got into trouble
When he went through all the bins
And ran into a busy road
To collect some shiny things.

The adults would tell Jasper
"That's dirty, put it down,"
And
"It's rubbish, sharp and dangerous,
Look, it's rusty, see, it's brown."

Jasper knew that it was rust
Because, as his book described,
Its chemicals had reacted
And created iron oxide.

Inside a rotting wooden box
He hid the things that glittered.

Which to anyone but Jasper
Looked just like dirty litter.

Jasper sometimes found it hard
To understand what had been said,
To put himself in others' shoes,
Or into someone else's head.

But those who aren't like Jasper
Have a problem much the same:

For how can they jump into
Jasper's unique brain?

Then one evening, late at night,
He heard his father say:

"He gets more like a magpie
With every passing day.
I'm worried he likes metals
More than having mates.
I don't want him to be the boy
Who's weird or people hate."

His parents talked for hours and hours,
And still they had some doubt

About what they could try to do
To help young Jasper out.

Next day, when he came home from school,
He could not believe his eyes.
On his plate were waffle sandwiches,
And cheese and baked bean pies.

Jasper thought it very strange
To have his favourite food
One whole week before his birthday –
but he still sat down to chew.

"Now, Jasper, we must ask you:
Can we help tidy up your box?
We know you love your shiny things,
But they smell worse than Dad's socks!
Look, these blocks are much more fun
For a boy who is your age,"

But Jasper had stopped listening,
And smashed his plate in rage.

Jasper ran around the house,
Kicking all the chairs.

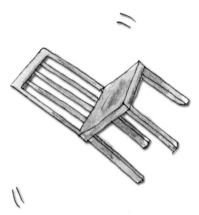

He messed up his parents' bedroom,
And threw things down the stairs.

He shouted words, so loudly,
that were not nice to hear,

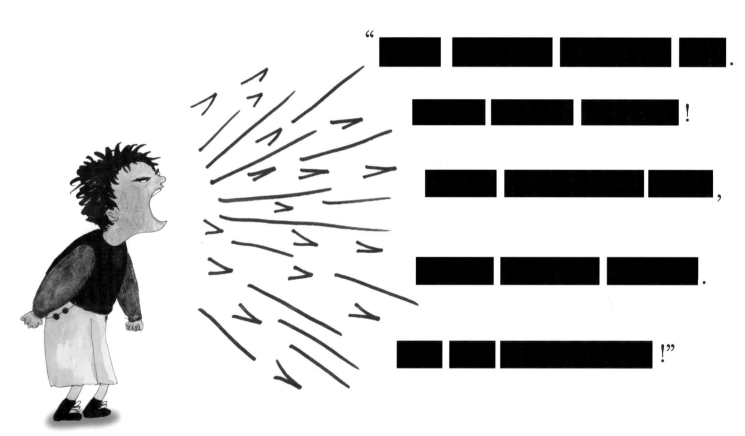

And surely would not be allowed
to be typed and printed here.

"I wish I was a magpie!
Then I'd fly away from you,
And collect my shiny metals,
And not get told what I should do!"

"These stupid blocks aren't alloys!
They are dull, and can't conduct.
These bricks are not reflective,
Or made of shiny stuff."

The whole next week he felt so bad,
And found it hard to sleep.

He was sad, confused, and sorry
And did not want to eat.

His mum and dad felt awful
To see him so upset.

And wondered what they could have done
Differently instead.

On the day that was his birthday,
His grandparents came to tea.

There was Gran who smelt of soil,

And Nan who smelt like peas.

Jasper liked to see them –
They were very old and kind,
And listened to him talk about
The things that he would find.

They said to him that everyone,
Including Dad and Mum,
Just wanted Jasper happy,
And not down or feeling glum.

Nan said that his birthday
Would be lots and lots of fun.
And Jasper gave a little smile,
Delighting everyone.

Then Gran said, *"Wait a minute,"*
So he counted, by the door,
All the way to sixty:

*"Elephant one, elephant two,
elephant three, elephant four...*

...elephant

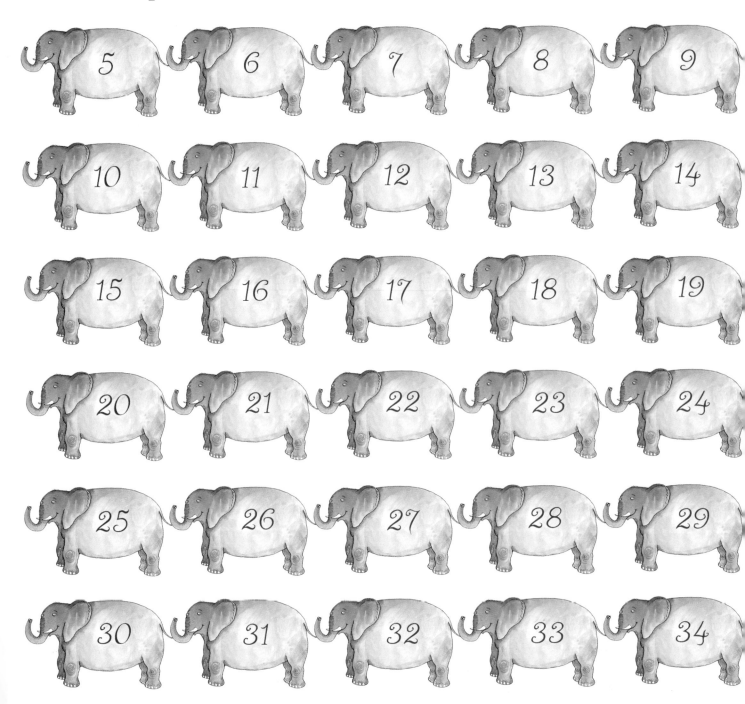

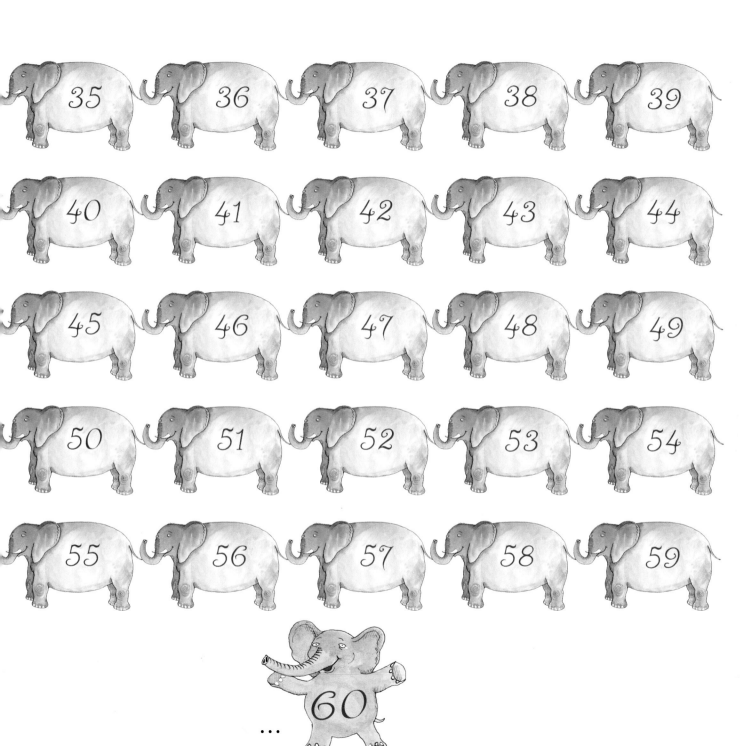

They presented him a parcel
All wrapped up in shiny paper,
With a bow of ductile copper
Which he saved to inspect later.

Inside the great big gift
Was a roll of kitchen foil,
And inside he also saw
A brilliant mirror ball.

His mum and dad decided,
After thinking for so long,
That Jasper's love of shiny things
Was not so very wrong.

So they'd saved up lots of wrappers,
Packets, foil and bottle tops,
And gave them as a present
In a big steel metal box.

TO OUR LITTLE MAGPIE
TRY TO SMILE AND NOT BE SAD
WE LIKE THAT YOU LIKE SHINY THINGS
WITH LOVE FROM

MUM and DAD

And inside Jasper also found:

A book of British birds,

A jumper with a magpie on,

And a pot of paint unstirred.

"With all your lovely shiny things
Here's something we could do:
We could draw a giant magpie
Then stick them down with glue."

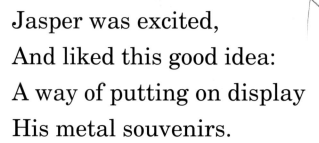

Jasper was excited,
And liked this good idea:
A way of putting on display
His metal souvenirs.

So Dad held out the paint pot,
And Mum passed him the brush,
And Jasper drew a magpie
Sitting on a little bush.

And in the great big magpie
They all stuck down shiny things
And covered its whole body –
Its head, its tail and wings.

The End

About the author and illustrator

Dan Mayfield is a writer and musician who has worked with people of all ages on the autism spectrum for over 12 years. His work continues to influence his ideas around what we as a society deem to be 'normal', and he has written this book to explore the importance of accepting other people's differences. Dan lives in London, UK.

Alex Merry is an illustrator and musician from Stroud in Gloucestershire. Her eye for the quirky and love of human difference informs her artwork. She is a committed, bell-jingling Morris dancer who performs in the UK and Europe.